SANTA BABY

Daryl-Jarod Entertainment
www.daryljarod.com

This is a work of fiction. The characters are fictional and any resemblance to actual persons, living or dead, is purely coincidental.

Manufactured in the United States of America

Cover Design by James, GoOnWrite.com

First Trade Paperback Edition December 2017

ISBN: 978-1-945748-05-9 (pbk)
ISBN: 978-1-945748-06-6 (ebook)

SANTA BABY

DARYL-JAROD

I dedicate this book to the most caring and extraordinary woman I know.
Not only that, the best mother I could've ever asked for.
Here's a Christmas story just for you!

Praise to be to God for giving me a sound mind and ever-flowing ideas to help this project blossom from an idea to a completed book.

I'd like to send a tremendous thank you to my beta readers; Casey, Amber, Anthony, Tori, Allie, Jomane, and Alyssa! You guys rock!

DECEMBER 22nd

11:34 A.M.

Joy! Joy!"

I turned around to face my manager, Tabitha, who was snapping her dusty fingers in my face.

"Huh? What?"

That job was so boring that I drifted off into vivid thoughts of how beautiful Christmas would be if it snowed for a change. I didn't care to have a few sprinkles here and there. I wanted a full-blown winter wonderland.

That wasn't very likely though. I lived in the south, where if it did snow, it was nothing worth bragging about. I needed to spend Christmas somewhere other than South Carolina, like New York or Michigan, if I wanted snow galore.

"Stop daydreaming and get back to work. I don't pay you to stand around and look pretty."

Tabitha scowled at me with an intense expression that warned me not to try her today. I didn't care. I just stared right back, giving her a hint not to test my patience either. I'd already had a lousy day before I stepped foot inside that awful place. I didn't need her on my back about that job. I was over that job!

"Look, Tabitha," I tried to explain.

"No, you look," she spat, rolling her eyes up to the ceiling and continuing to put her hands in my face.

I instantly thought about pulling that index finger and breaking it. Maybe then she'd get the picture that I did not care to be bothered.

"When I hired you, something told me you weren't going to be hard worker. Something told me that."

To be such a gorgeous woman, Tabitha had the ugliest attitude. She was Arabic, standing at about five-six, with long jet black hair and intoxicating light brown eyes.

Her exterior was runway model ready, but that interior needed a full-blown makeover, pronto.

"Oh, really?" I took a step backward, just so I could have my personal space. Otherwise, I feared I'd have no choice but to smack the daylights out of her. "Then why did you hire me?"

"Get. Back. To. Work."

Tabitha gave me one more eye roll before she spun around and fiercely stormed away.

I huffed, as I rolled my eyes as well. That woman was about to literally bring out a part of myself I chose to not expose within the work place. And it appeared that I was the only employee she chose to continually pester about little things. Just thirty minutes prior, she was on my case about how I handed our customers their change the improper way. An hour before that, she was on my back about my natural hair, suggesting I change it to appear like everyone else's.

I was the only black woman working in that store. I refused to wear a wig or have to flat iron my lusciously long afro, just to please Tabitha or anyone for that matter. Wearing my hair exactly as it was would have to do.

Yes, Tabitha had a major storm coming her way, by the name of hurricane Joy, if she didn't get a clue and leave me be. I just had to do my best to hold off on losing my cool until after the holiday season. Tabitha's father, Abdul, owned the store and if I even breathed the wrong way, she was in daddy's office to complain about me.

I had only been working there for about a month, but in that short time, I'd already had many, many days where I had to coach myself out of quitting. Yes, I needed the money. But at the end of the day, that job was beneath me.

And no, I absolutely am not bad mouthing anyone who actually enjoys a job that has you standing at a cash register for an entire shift. It's all good. Do you. We all have to do what makes us happy.

But I was a college graduate. I majored in

musical theatre, with a minor in business administration. While the majority of my peers were out partying and drinking the night away, I was locked up in my room, studying to remain on top of the Dean's List. There was not a single class I didn't excel in. On top of that, I had a freaking plan for my life and what I'd be doing after graduation. But very quickly, I learned how things don't always go the way we envision them.

I found a nice entry-level job at a local theatre immediately after college. I wasn't performing on stage, but working as their stage technician was a start in the right direction.

Things were swell there, up until my boss made it clear that I'd have to sleep with him in order to move up in the company. I quit and the months that followed consisted of me working a series of jobs unrelated to my major.

I then fell in love with a man who made my heart sing. That man was everything I'd ever prayed, hoped, and dreamed of…and then some. He filled my head with sweet nothings, claiming he wanted marriage and a lifetime together. But just as soon as I got knocked up, he ran for the hills.

Not long after, I found a job I believed would be impossible for a girl like me to ever snag. When your best friend's husband is CEO of an up-and-booming investment company and he's well aware of your skill assets, it's an easy win.

Still, I wasn't putting all the blood, sweat, and tears that came from working my butt off to earn that degree, to use in the job market. However, I found the pay raise that came along with the title of a Benefits Consultant, to be well worth it. At least it was for the moment.

I worked there for six years and during that time, I knew everything in life could only continue to get better from there.

I was wrong. Dead wrong.

Apparently, my best friend's husband, Tucker, was involved in some sort of drug business and the FBI took his whole company down and him as well. My best friend, Rachel, fell into a deep depression and thought it was best to end our decade-long friendship. She informed me that she no longer knew who to trust and my loyalty over the years just wasn't enough to hold the friendship together.

On top of dealing with that, I was jobless with a six-year-old son to care for. My options were limited since each job interview went nowhere and my savings were sadly diminishing as each month rolled on by.

Conveniently, one day I saw a help wanted ad in the window of a local toy store. I'd only gone inside the store because my son begged and pleaded. I admit I was cautious at first because the store was so empty. The employees outnumbered the customers. And not only that, it lacked a sense of liveliness.

I do think most of that could be blamed on location though. Tab's Toy barn had only been open for a few months, so they should've been booming with business. The store was, however, located on a poor side of town. With high priced toys and electronics, they couldn't have seriously expected people to dispose of their hard-earned money. Not when there was eBay and Amazon.

To add more fuel to the fire, those dingy floors, with a ceiling that looked like it'd collapse at any moment, were enough to send any new customer flying out the door. And don't get me started on the unpleasant odor that reminded me of wet paint.

With all that being said, my intuition warned me that working there would be the ultimate snooze fest. But I applied nevertheless.

And that was that.

One week later, I was hired at Tab's Toy Barn and unhappy as ever. I still had much to be thankful for. I had clothes on my back, my family and my heartbeat; my son JJ.

But still…no matter how much I focused on the positive, nothing could change how much that job sucked!

"You okay, sunshine?" my co-worker, Wade, asked as he approached the register next to me and signed on.

"I'm good. How are you, Wade?"

"I'm fantastic, babe. But I'd be even better when you let me take you out. Let me show ya how a real man can take care of a fine lady, like yourself."

"Ugh, Wade. Stop it, please."

Wade was the complete opposite of the type of guy I'd go for. He was in his late sixties, with a beer belly, unkempt facial hair that was completely gray and huge bifocals that should've been abandoned in the eighties.

I'd already expressed exactly how uninterested I was, daily. But my words appeared to not faze him as he ignored the rejection. He must've been under the impression that I'd give in if he didn't give up.

I felt the need to remind him, so I said, "Wade, you have no chance with me. You're a nice guy, but you're old enough to be my father, maybe even my grandfather."

I understood why he found interest in me. Men had no shame in expressing how they admired the freckles upon my face, my naturally red-hued hair, and how they were in lust with my smooth caramel-colored skin. To add the cherry on top, let's not forget about their rude comments referring to my curvy hips and banging body for a woman with a kid.

There were undoubtedly always rude comments men somehow believed to be compliments to my ego. Those corny pickup lines would get them nowhere. It was a habit turning them down left and right. I had no interest in dating. My main priority as a mother was taking care of JJ.

"Age ain't nothing but a number, sunshine." I cringed. There was nothing cute about him referring to me as anything other than my actual name. "Come on, sunshine. Let me take you out and show you things real men can do."

"And what exactly would that be?" A voice approached us from behind. It was Abdul. "Go ahead and tell me, Wade. I'll wait."

Wade was speechless for once. "Well, I...I was only saying-"

"How about you don't. This is a workplace. My workplace and I need you to not assault your coworkers."

Abdul was a short man; about five-foot-three or five-foot-four. Compared to Wade's over six-foot stature, he was nothing more than a tiny ant. But his height did not get in the way of him taking charge of any and every situation that occurred in his store. We were all aware that he played no games when it came down to work.

"I wasn't assaulting her boss. I was-"

He held up his hands to silence Wade's lies. "Just stop. We need to have another chat." He turned his attention to me. "Joy, can I get you to start stocking our new shipment?"

I nodded, "Of course." And then

mouthed him a thank you.

Tabitha probably complained about my attitude, so he had no choice but to come see what I was up to. Good thing he did. Wade was a little too much to deal with.

"Let me ask you this," I heard him say to Wade as I walked away slowly. "Do you really want to keep your job?"

I smirked, knowing Wade would deny ever bothering me or any other woman at work.

When I arrived to the stock room, Tabitha was exiting. She made a sly smirk my way, then walked out. My coworker, Melanie, told me not to stress it, as she unboxed the latest gaming craze kids all over the world were dying to have for Christmas.

It was the Amega X, widely referred to as the ultimate gaming system. Doubtful that the statement lived up to its gaming performance, I did tons of research on it. Barely even one bad review online. People raved it was the best console of the generation.

With capabilities that exceeded anything in stores at the moment, it was a no-brainer why so many kids, and adults, were fighting hard to get their hands on the device, which had limited stock everywhere.

JJ was no exception. He asked me on a daily basis if he'd be getting it for Christmas. I always told him not to count on it, since money was so tight. As expensive as the Amega was, five hundred bucks to be exact, I knew for sure he wouldn't be getting it. It was going to break my heart to see him so disappointed on Christmas morning.

"Girl, you good?" Melanie asked, after standing up and touching my shoulder.

I nodded, then stated, "Oh yeah. I'm fine."

"Well, if you need to talk, I'm here."

I thanked her, but knew very well I'd never go to her, or anyone else for that matter, for help with my life problems.

7:02 P.M.

Mommy, today was such a good day," JJ cheerfully told me, as he chowed down on Mickey D's french fries in the backseat.

I laughed and glanced back into the rearview mirror. "Oh really, sweetheart? Why's that?"

"'Cause today CeCe kissed me, and you brought me food!"

"Whoa, whoa! What?" I asked, through amusement and laughter. "CeCe gave you a what?"

"A kiss," he smiled. "And she put it right here." He placed a greasy fingertip upon his cheek and smiled up at me, showing a mouthful of unswallowed french fries.

"Chew your food, JJ." He closed his mouth as I continued, "And why did she kiss you?"

"'Cause she's my girlfriend."

Now, that really made me chuckle. It was cute. I recalled having my first playground "boyfriend". It was fun and innocent, but like all children, I had no idea what real love was.

"Ohhh, your girlfriend, huh?" I teased.

He eagerly nodded his head. "We love each other."

"Oh, you do?"

"Yes, Mommy."

"But not more than you love Mommy?"

His face frowned in the same way mine would if I'd just heard something purely ridiculous. He had so many of my traits and mannerisms, from his skin complexion to the way his dimples accompanied his smile.

But still, he was the spitting image of his father. Dark brown eyes, handsome face and a big head. They even shared the same odd hairline.

For the first year of JJ's life, I couldn't look at him without reminiscing over his deadbeat father and all the unnecessary stress I had to endure with him. As a result of that, I picked up the habit of referring to my son as JJ, and not Jeffrey Jr.

"No, Mommy. I'll always love you more. You are my everything."

I laughed to prevent myself from becoming emotional. That little boy knew how to tug on my heartstrings. He was my everything as well. He always would be.

"Does my daddy love me too?"

And there was that dreaded conversation again. It was a conversation that made me pray to the heavens above for it to not occur often.

How do you tell a child that his father

wants nothing at all to do with him? I tried time and time again to get that man involved in his son's life. He wasn't having it. He blocked me on Facebook, Twitter, Instagram and went so far as changing his number and moving apartments.

I assumed me showing up to his apartment with my fed-up mom and aunt was just too much for him to handle. I had no regrets. I hadn't brought JJ into the world by myself. So why was I supporting him *by myself*?

After two years of attempting to help a boy transition into a man, I gave up. He clearly did not want to be bothered and I was well aware I'd be a better father and mother to my son anyway. I didn't need him and JJ wouldn't either. He'd have other father figures in his life, like my dad and uncles, to show him how to be a better man than his father.

"Why do you ask that, JJ?"

He looked down at the food in his lap, which was a complete mess. I'd have to vacuum the entire backseat when we got home.

"JJ, what made you ask that?"

"All my friends talk about their daddies…and, and what they do. But I don't know my daddy."

He looked up at me with tears in his eyes and I found myself having to look away as the tears began to escape from mine as well.

We rarely spoke about his father, but I was aware that as he grew older he'd have more questions. I did my best to prepare for that dreaded conversation. However, no matter how hard I attempted to, it didn't make it one bit easier.

"Baby, you know I'll always be honest with you." I took a second to compose the right words, then continued, "Yes, you do have a father. Where he is...I don't know. But you do have me. And I promise I will always do my very best to provide for you and make sure you have everything you need." The tears continued to fall as my voice began to crack. "And you have grandpa, who's always there for you, no matter what."

"I know, Mommy."

My words weren't enough to put his little heart at ease. I did my best. Still, it wasn't good enough.

"Don't cry, Mommy. I'm sorry."

I wiped away my tears. It was time to be a big girl, at least on the outside.

"Oh no, baby. You don't have to be sorry. You wanted to know."

He gazed out the window and I focused on the road, occasionally sneaking peeks in the rearview mirror at him.

After a moment of silence, I asked, "You wanna listen to Fetty Wap?"

He looked up at me and quickly nodded.

I strolled through the tunes on my iPhone, then pressed PLAY for Fetty Wap's "My

Way"…the clean non-explicit version, of course. I turned up the volume a couple notches as the catchy song began to play.

JJ began to dance along to his favorite song. I followed suit by bopping my head and singing along to the tune.

In that moment, things were fine. They wouldn't always be. JJ would return another day, maybe a year later with more questions. And in my heart, I knew I'd still never be ready for it.

7:31 P.M.

It was a spur of the moment idea, but I decided to swing by my parents' place before officially heading home. It seemed only right that JJ see my dad and I speak with my mom about our conversation in the car.

JJ looked up from his PSP as I turned off the car engine. "We seeing grandma and grandpa?"

I nodded. He then dropped his hand-held game system to the floor and jetted out of the car in a hurry.

My mom opened the front door and greeted her favorite, and only, grandson.

I got out of the car, then briskly walked to the front door, pulling my jacket around my body as tightly as possible. It was freezing outside! I absolutely loved living in South Carolina, but I was not thrilled about the cold winter months. I could not wait until summer rolled around.

I could feel myself becoming a bit more cheerful though, as I admired my parents' home. Fully decked with Christmas lights and a yard complete with holiday decorations, it was the coziest and most beautiful two-story home I'd ever laid eyes on. And that statement could be totally biased, since I at one point lived there.

My parents purchased the house when I was just a baby, so there were so many childhood memories there. No matter how old I got, I could always come back, go into my old bedroom, and reminisce about the past.

A smile appeared to my face as I watched JJ and my mom hug. He loved his grandma to pieces and in return she'd do anything for him.

It brought my troubled heart much solace being able to see my mom. We didn't always get along, but at the end of the day she was still my mother and I'd always love her unconditionally.

Mama kissed JJ's forehead, then looked up at me with a warm smile. She'd just turned sixty-four three weeks prior, but she'd aged gracefully.

With her long salt and pepper hair pulled back into a ponytail, her high cheek bones and bright eyes were prominent and able to shine. She didn't look a day over forty-five, which gave me hope that I'd look just as good at her age.

"Grandma, how'd you know we were here?"

"Oh, Grandma always knows these things, sugar," Mom informed him with a smile.

"You were peeking out the window again, weren't you?" I asked, already knowing the truth.

"Oh, girl hush!" Mama said, pulling me in for a hug.

She held onto me for a few seconds, which was nice, since I hadn't seen her in about three weeks. Our daily phone conversations were down to about once a week. I blamed it on a busy work schedule, but I was barely working as it was. I was simply too prideful and ashamed of anyone knowing what was going on. JJ was the only person who actually knew I was no longer working at the investment company.

"I missed you," she whispered in my ear.

"I missed you, too..."

Mama placed a sweet kiss on my cheek and then we followed behind JJ, who led the way inside.

"Is that Joy?" asked a voice I recognized right away.

I entered the kitchen to find my Aunt Joyce sitting at the kitchen table with a cup in her hands, and a bottle of eggnog accompanied with a bottle of Vodka, all lined up in front of her. From the looks of the Vodka bottle, there was surely more alcohol than eggnog in her cup.

"Auntie Joyce!" I exclaimed, as I extended my arms for a hug.

She placed her cup down, then pushed out her chair as an effort to stand.

"No, no, don't worry about getting up."

I wrapped my arms around her and took

in her scent. She smelled like sugar cookies and too much perfume; the combination of scents that could only be my lively Aunt Joyce.

"Okay, now. I need for all of you to stop treating me like I'm old and handicapped."

"Hush, Joyce!" Mama said, as she gestured for me to sit down. "Nobody ever said you was all of that."

I sat down at the table, with JJ on my lap, as I watched my mom and her only sister go back and forth. They always argued. If they didn't argue, there was something clearly wrong.

It was all out of love and just their way of bonding with one another. No matter what happened in life, they still each other's backs.

My mom was there for every minute of Aunt Joyce's turbulent marriage. Dad even told me she once jumped on Aunt Joyce's ex-husband when she got word of how he'd put his hands on her.

And Aunt Joyce was there for Mama throughout her rough pregnancy with me. She helped deliver me when her water broke at a relative's home. The doctors said Aunt Joyce helped save my life and Mama's life as well, with all of her knowledge as a nurse. For that reason, I was named Joy.

Knowing that I'd survive brought Mama more joy than she ever could've imagined. She also wanted to pay homage to how grateful she'd been to her sister, by giving me a name similar to hers.

"Mommy, I'm hungry," JJ told me, not interested in the back and forth arguing taking place before him.

"JJ, you just ate."

"Let the boy eat," said Mama and Aunt Joyce in unison.

We all laughed as Mama handed JJ a Lunchables package from the fridge. She kept those on deck for situations like this when her grandbabies needed a snack.

"Go ahead and go in the living room, baby," Mama told him, as she kissed his forehead.

He hopped off of my lap, but I held onto his hand.

"The living room? Mama, you know JJ can make a mess."

"Don't worry about that. JJ, go in the living room."

JJ glanced at me, then Mama, and eventually decided to listen to his grandma. I assume he figured he might as well do it there because it'd never happen at home.

I found it funny how Mama was carefree with him, with all of her grandchildren. If that had been me or my sister, Ebony, she would shut that down in a heartbeat.

As Mama joined us at the table, I asked, "So, where's Daddy?"

"He went out to the liquor store. He should be back soon."

I shook my head and laughed. If Daddy was out to get alcohol and Auntie Joyce was around, that only meant one thing. It was about to be a fun, intoxicating night for the both of them.

Without fail, they always had a good time together. Mama usually let them be as they trash talked, drank, and played spades. It kept my aunt off her back and she could focus on reading or her crocheting.

"Why?" Mama asked. "What's going on, Joy?"

"Oh, nothing. I just wanted to speak to him and say hey."

"Girl, stop lying to your mama," Aunt Joyce spoke up. "We both knew something was wrong the moment you walked in here. I can just see that pain in your face, girl."

They probably could sense that there was something bothering me. After all, they'd known me my entire life. I was quite talented at withholding the truth about things going on in my life, but I was awful at hiding my emotions.

I decided to skip the part about me losing my job and how I was now working at the toy store. "On the way home from daycare, JJ asked if his dad loves him. I did my best. But I feel like it'd be good for him to see daddy for a bit before we head home."

"That loser," Aunt Joyce remarked, after taking a gulp of eggnog. "I still wish you'd let me slash his tires. If he don't wanna be a father, he should've never laid down with you to begin with."

"I'm glad you didn't do that, Auntie Joyce. It would've only worsened the situation."

Mama then spoke up. "I do think it'd be good for JJ to spend more time with his grandpa. You know your dad always wanted a boy to go do manly things with."

"Yeah, I think Daddy would like that as well."

She placed a hand on top of mine, then said, "Why don't you let us watch JJ during the day. Both me and your dad are now retired and I'm sure he'll do a good job of keeping us busy. I know you don't need to save any money with that good job and all, but we'd love to help out."

"Let them help you, Joy," Aunt Joyce chimed in.

I laughed, "I wasn't going to say no, this time."

Both Mama and Daddy had offered a few times in the past to look after JJ, and I declined. I didn't want help from anyone. JJ was my offspring and I felt that I could handle it all alone.

But things can change in the blink of an eye. I needed their help now more than ever.

"Ah, there's my baby girl."

I turned my head and couldn't help but smile as my favorite man entered the room. The one man who hadn't broken my heart and would do anything at all to keep a smile on my face.

"Daddy!" I exclaimed, as I shot up from the table and ran over to him.

"Baby girl!" he said, just as excited as I was.

I got a good look at Daddy before we embraced. He looked vibrant, cheerful, and content. I assumed his recent retirement aided in doing his body some good. His normally tired and red eyes now appeared to be refreshed.

It made my heart sing being able to witness his happiness. And the same for Mama.

He was sporting his usual causal wear; a polo shirt that was fitted, but not too snug, along with khaki pants and white sneakers. His favorite baseball cap sat upon his head, hiding his mixture of red and gray strands.

"Look at these two," Aunt Joyce remarked, laughing with Mama.

"Grandpa! Grandpa!" JJ cried, running in from the living room and into the kitchen.

He tripped on a step and fell face down onto the kitchen tile. Daddy and I rushed over to him, with Mama and Aunt Joyce right behind.

It took a second for JJ to feel the pain and when it hit him, he began to holler.

Daddy picked him up in his arms and

began to soothe him by rocking him back and forth. "There, there. You're okay, little man. You're okay."

I inspected his face and arms. No bruises or blood to be found. I joined Mama and Aunt Joyce at the table as we watched Daddy bond with JJ.

I grinned at the thought of how my parents spoiled him. It could've been due to the fact that they rarely saw my sister's two daughters. Either way, JJ would always feel loved in the presence of his grandparents.

"Boy almost gave me a heart attack," joked Aunt Joyce.

"Well, nobody told you to get up the way you did. You shouldn't be moving around at all. You need to be in bed resting."

Aunt Joyce waved Mama off. "Oh, stop it."

"You hear these two old women arguing?" Daddy joked to a now calm JJ. He wiped away JJ's tears. "Tell them to stop arguing."

"Stop it," JJ said weakly.

We all laughed, which helped to put a big smile on his face.

"I missed you, Grandpa," JJ said, once Daddy placed him down to stand. He hugged onto his leg, then continued, "I gotta tell you all about my girlfriend."

"Girlfriend?" asked Daddy and Mama at

the same time.

JJ nodded. "And I love her. And did you know Mommy works at my favorite toy store now and she's getting the toy I want for Christmas?"

"JJ," I snapped, as everyone's attention was now focused on me.

"What's he talking about, Joy?" Mama questioned. "Why are you working at a toy store?"

"'Cause she don't have her other job anymore," JJ added.

I placed a hand on my forehead. "JJ, please."

"No," Daddy begun. "Maybe he should continue."

Mama chimed in, "Yeah, because he's telling us stuff I had no idea about."

Aunt Joyce took a deep sigh and then emptied the entirety of the Vodka into her cup. I was pretty sure she was drinking straight Vodka at that point.

"Do we really have to talk about this, guys?"

It wasn't that I was hell bent on keeping secrets from my family. I simply did not care to discuss it. I was a grown woman handling my business the best way I knew how.

"We surely do," Mama snapped with a stern look that made me so uncomfortable, I had to look away.

"Come on, JJ," Daddy said, picking him up into his arms and giving me a sympathetic look. He knew Mama was about to dig into me until she got every detail. "Let's go watch TV."

"Sorry, Mommy," JJ whispered, as they exited the room.

"What happened, Joy?" Mama asked. I could sense she was trying not to be upset.

"Nothing, Mama. Just drop it."

"I will not. Now tell me what happened. I know it's not acting or singing, but at least the money was good, Joy. Why'd you leave that good job? Did you get fired? Oh God, Joy! What did you do?"

"Mama, please! Relax. Let me explain."

I took a moment to close my eyes and when I opened them, both Mama and Aunt Joyce were staring impatiently at me.

"Okay...so, here's what happened..."

I took my time to explain every single detail to them. I didn't need to tell part of the truth and then have to explain why I wasn't completely honest to begin with. I informed them how my former boss and his affiliates were now behind bars, the business taken down, and how I struggled for almost three months just living off my savings because I couldn't find work.

"What? I need to call Rachel right now and see what she can do for you. There's gotta be something."

I insisted, "Mama, please do not call Rachel."

"Why not? She is your best friend, isn't she? With her husband in jail, she's probably off to start some other business. You know that girl is always doing something."

I didn't care to linger on with a conversation about Rachel, so I bluntly stated, "We aren't friends anymore. That's over and done with. And things won't ever be the same."

Mama paused, then blinked a few times, and replied, "Over ten years of friendship and it's over? Why?"

"It just is."

She began to shake her head. "I just don't understand, Joy. You should've told us. We would've helped you."

"I know. I didn't want any help."

She looked away from me, then looked to Aunt Joyce. Surprisingly, my aunt remained silent.

"Fine," she finally stated. "We're helping you now. I know you won't accept any money from us because you're just that stubborn, but we *will* help you with JJ. No more daycare until you can afford it."

I nodded, with no backlash.

I was thankful she cared so much and also thankful I had one less bill to worry about.

11:06 P.M.

I'd just managed to close my eyes and drift off to sleep when I received a phone call from my sister, Ebony.

"Yes," I answered, sleepily into the phone.

"What's this I hear about you working at that toy barn?"

I exhaled a sigh of regret for even going over to my parents' house to begin with. I sat up against the headboard, and replied, "Well, hello to you too, Ebony."

"Hey, now tell me what's going on?"

"Didn't you already hear all of this from Mama?"

Those two on the phone together were nothing but gossip queens.

"Yeah, I did. But I wanna hear it from you!"

"Look. I gotta get up early in the morning for work, so we'll have to finish this conversation later."

"No, no, we won't. We will talk about this right now."

There she went again, believing she could

Daryl-Jarod

talk to me like she was my parent. She'd always been that way. Just because she was ten years older, she continued to think she had the right to tell me how to live.

"What about JJ? What kind of example are you setting for him as a mother?"

And that's when I snapped. "I'm sorry. Who do you think you are, trying to tell me how to raise my son? You don't even have custody of your own kids, so I don't want to hear it."

"How dare you speak to-"

"Goodbye."

I hung up the phone and went right to sleep, satisfied that she'd lose sleep because I pissed her off.

DECEMBER 23rd

5:30 A.M.

Once again, it felt like as soon as I'd closed my eyes, it was time to get up. I found myself growing accustomed to it, though. And my daily reasoning for waking up so early was just so I could hit the gym and relieve all my pent-up stress.

Luckily, my parents only lived ten minutes away from my house, so I was able to drop JJ off with them in a hurry.

"But I wanna stay home today, Mommy," JJ whined when we arrived to my parents' place.

"No, you're staying here until I get off work."

He whined, but he'd soon get over it. He was adamant about staying home alone, so he could prove to me how much of a big boy he was. But I was sure he'd quit whining and fall fast asleep as soon as his head hit the pillow in my parent's soft king-sized bed.

I didn't like the idea of leaving him home alone anyway. If he had a sibling or one of his cousins to be there with him, I'd be more open to the idea. In the day and age we lived in, there was no way I'd ever leave my son home without supervision.

"Have a good day at work," Mama told me, as I hugged both her and JJ goodbye.

She appeared to be over the conversation we'd had several hours prior. My dad most likely said something to her about leaving me be.

"Thanks. Love you guys."

I got back into my car, cranked up the heat and sang along to Mariah Carey's classic tune, "All I Want for Christmas."

6:01 A.M.

The Christmas songs continued on through my headphones, as I sprinted on the treadmill, pushing my body to blast away the calories I consumed earlier that morning. This time I chose to jam to a new Christmas song by Sia, entitled, "Santa's Coming for Us".

The gym was packed, which I didn't find the least bit surprising. It was a Saturday, after all. Everyone probably got up extra early so they could burn a few calories and then hit the stores to finish their last-minute Christmas shopping.

Me, on the other hand, would be at work, having to deal with agitating Tabitha and overbearing Wade.

"Ughhh!" I shrieked aloud, increasing my speed on the treadmill.

If JJ's bum of a father hadn't been so selfish and only out for himself, I surely wouldn't be in my current predicament. JJ also would've most definitely had a Christmas to look forward to.

Last time I checked, Jeffrey was still boasting on social media about all the expensive

Daryl-Jarod

shoes and watches he had. If he was so well off, and if he even had a heart, he'd help out for the sake of his son.

"He should be ashamed of himself!" I blurted, now huffing and puffing.

He was the root of all my anger. He was the reason why I hadn't been with another man since he disappeared. Because of him I wouldn't entertain the thought of dating, let alone dreaming of a future with someone.

"I can't believe he did this to me!"

I was now running so fast that my body was screaming for me to stop and give it a moment of rest. People were beginning to stare and point at me, as well. I wasn't fazed. They had no idea what I was going through. If they'd experienced the same ordeal as me, they be almost at a breaking point as well.

He promised me marriage, I thought to myself. *He promised me a future!*

The sudden stop of the treadmill made my body fall forward. Luckily, there was a body that grabbed onto me to prevent a drastic fall.

"Maybe you should take a break from the treadmill," said a charming voice that came directly from the stranger who saved me.

I was still trying to process it all. What stopped the treadmill to begin with?

Then I looked down to discover his hands were holding onto my arms. His feet were positioned on the side of the treadmill's running belt, legs wide open. For the very first time in a while, I had to admit it felt lovely to be touched by a man.

I spun around, releasing myself from his magical touch. Staring down at me was a man so deliciously attractive, I had to blink several times to ensure I hadn't been dreaming.

"Are you okay?" he asked, with a worrisome expression. "I think everyone here is a little concerned.

"I'm not worried about what anyone here thinks," I admitted, placing a hand on his chest to lightly push him back.

I allowed my hand to remain there a second longer. Just from the area I touched, it was evident this guy lived in the gym. My eyes roamed all over his chest and abs, which showed through his muscle shirt.

"That's understandable." He backed up, got off the treadmill, and then hopped onto the one directly next to me. "I was just making sure you were okay."

"Well, thank you for that."

The handsome stranger began to walk at a slow pace, while I pondered on the events that had just transpired. If he hadn't stopped me when he did, who knows what would've happened. I could've overworked myself so much that someone would've been forced to call an ambulance.

I should've been grateful instead of angry

with his actions.

"Thanks again. That was kind of you."

"Don't sweat it. You just looked like you needed a break," he laughed.

"I think you made the right decision," I replied, starting the treadmill at a much slower pace this time.

He looked over at me like I was crazy.

"I promise to just walk from now on."

He chuckled, "Please, let that be all you do."

I got lost in his eyes for a moment and almost tripped again from his dreamy presence.

"You good?"

I nodded. "Of course. Of course."

"Alright now. Don't end up breaking your legs just from walking."

"That would be awful."

"Agreed."

I bit my tongue and thought for a good minute before I decided to introduce myself. With it being so long since I'd even attempted to flirt with a man, I was surely rusty. He was fine though. I at least had to say something.

"I'm Joy."

"Nick." He extended his hand and shook mine. "It's nice to meet you, Joy."

"Oh, the pleasure is all mine," I said in a suggestive tone that even surprised myself.

He grinned, then glanced down at the meter on his treadmill. I was prepared to continue the conversation and find out more about him, but the ringing of my phone distracted me.

It was Tabitha. For the life of me, I couldn't figure out what she wanted so early in the morning. I wasn't scheduled to work for another three hours. I didn't answer. Whatever it was, it could wait until I arrived to work.

"So, do you come to this gym often, Nick?"

I looked over to see Nick was nowhere to be found. It was the strangest thing. One second he was right beside me and then the next, gone. The treadmill had stopped and there was no evidence left behind that suggested he'd even been there. I was beginning to think I'd imagined everything. Maybe, I was so lonely I had to dream up a man?

I glanced down at my phone and frowned at the text message from Tabitha. She needed me to work as soon as possible.

After debating for the next few moments, I got off the treadmill and prepared to go home and shower. Apparently, I wasn't getting very much exercise done, so I might as well have gone into work early. My paycheck would thank me later.

7:45 A.M.

Not even ten minutes into my shift and the thought of leaving crossed my mind for what felt like the thousandth time. I was mentally over it.

The store was dead. No surprise there. We only had two customers in the store and they didn't appear interested in purchasing anything. They just walked around aimlessly, occasionally stopping to look at something.

Tabitha was on my case, as usual, forcing me to follow them around and ask if they had any questions about any item.

"You know what, that's it. I do not need any help and I don't appreciate you guys constantly following me around," said an Asian guy who was about twenty-one years of age or so.

He kept eyeing our overpriced video games. I was willing to bet that if we sold our electronics at reasonable rates, he would've already racked up an armful of games.

"I'm so sorry, sir," I replied. "My manager just really wanted to make sure you found everything okay."

"Well, as I stated four times already. I don't need any help. Good luck getting any business with that strategy."

He briskly walked away from me and out of the store.

With only one other customer left, I decided not to follow the same route. That store needed to bring in more money or I'd be out of a job.

What I didn't understand was why Tabitha and Abdul never thought to hold a Black Friday sale. That could've at least brought in more profit for the end of November. Those two weren't trying to hear any suggestions or feedback. It was their way or the highway. And as much as I despised the place, I had to hold on a little longer until I found something else.

9:07 P.M.

It had been such an uneventful and dull day, but I still found myself feeling exhausted. After work, I picked up JJ and we went straight home. I fixed dinner while he watched Cartoon Network.

I should've known better than to let him watch that. A commercial for the Amega X came on during every commercial break, and of course, that night was no exception.

JJ looked over at the Christmas tree, then back at me. "Mommy, I don't see it under the tree."

"And how would you know if it's there or not. Everything is wrapped."

"Because I know, Mommy. I always can guess my presents."

He surely could. I had no choice but to start being creative by putting small gifts inside of huge boxes to try and throw off his inquisitive mind.

He continued, "I know all that's under the tree are clothes, so Santa must be bringing it to me, since you haven't got it yet."

I couldn't hold back a sigh, while he resumed watching television. As Christmas Day inched by closer, it only got harder. He wanted that game system more than anything in the world.

I'd tried to find it online, just to see if it were cheaper. Amazon, eBay, Toys R Us...they were all now sold out of it. Even if I had the money, there was no chance JJ would get it by Christmas.

We ate dinner, then I gave JJ a bath and kissed him goodnight. I then took a nice, relaxing bath and retired to my bed.

We'd all been informed the following day at work would be a busy one. I understood people would be doing some shopping to pick up a few last-minute gifts before Christmas, but no one cared to shop at our store.

I didn't expect a big turnout. Still, I closed my eyes and allowed my body to get some much-needed sleep.

DECEMBER 24th

11:32 A.M.

I was beyond shocked to see that Tabitha and Abdul's predictions were correct. In fact, busy was an understatement. The place was a freaking mad house!

They neglected to inform us that the store was holding a huge promotion, which meant all items in the store were half off. *Everything!*

As you can imagine, people were running around frantic and deranged, like a chicken with its head cut off. Parents were fighting over toys while their children cried. There were racks knocked over and nothing in place where it should've been. It wasn't even noon yet, so I feared things would only become more hectic from there.

To make matters worse, I checked out customer after customer, who purchased the Amega X. It was frustrating. Not only could I not purchase it for my son, I had to constantly witness other parents and grandparents purchase it, as well.

"My grandson is gonna be so happy to see this tomorrow," said a woman who appeared to be about seventy or so.

I scanned the console, told her the total, and then said, "I'm sure he will be. My son has been begging for this for months. It's just too expensive."

"It's half off right now, baby. Why don't you put one to the side before it sells out? Maybe just purchase it on your break?"

That idea hadn't crossed my mind. If it was half off, it still, was a little pricey in my opinion. But since JJ was dying to have it, I could put my newly frugal ways aside for once.

I finished our transaction, thanked the woman and told her to have a great day and a joyful Christmas.

"Oh, I'm sorry," I said to a man who appeared to be in a hurry, as he approached my register. "This register is temporarily closed. I'll be right back."

He gave me a look of annoyance and my coworkers all looked at me as though I'd bumped my head.

"I'll be right back," I repeated, then briskly walked away, leaving my coworkers to deal with the ridiculously-crazy line.

I did intend on returning as soon as I could. I simply had to do something that couldn't wait.

I found Tabitha in the breakroom, feet up on the table, with a magazine in her hand and a half-eaten apple in the other. It was no shocker that she was sitting on her behind relaxing, while we slaved away on the floor.

When her eyes made contact with mine, she shot up, dropping the magazine to the floor. "What? What happened? Are people fighting again?"

"No, no," I assured her. "Well, not yet anyway."

She gave me a nod, clearly relieved, then sat back down and picked up her magazine. "Then what is it?"

"I was just wondering if you'd mind if I put one of our consoles to the side. It's the one thing my son has his heart set on…and since it's half off I'd really be able to buy it. I'm afraid it'll be gone by the time I get off."

Tabitha stared at me for a second and then threw her head back in laughter. This went on for a few moments too long. For the life of me, I couldn't figure out what was so funny.

When her laughter subsided, she gave me a stern glare that was so cold. "Look, Joan, or whatever your name is…I don't know if you're aware of this or not, but this is a business we're trying to run, sweetie. I don't care about your son or what he wants for Christmas."

As she expressed how she truly felt, my mouth dropped open in disbelief of her nerve. I couldn't believe she was actually saying all of this…to my face! Don't get me wrong. Tabitha could be heartless and evil, but she'd never gone this far.

"How dare you step in here and try to make me feel pity for you," she continued, taking a bite of her apple and chewing with her mouth open.

"It's not my fault you can't afford a lousy toy. No, you cannot put it to the side to purchase later. And no, you can't buy it after work, even if we have one leftover."

"Tabitha, what-"

She interrupted me, holding her hand up and replying, "Enough! Get back on that floor, Joanna. We have money to make. And if you would like to keep your job, you'll do it...*now!*"

She then had the audacity to roll her eyes at me. Tabitha kicked her feet back up on the table and resumed reading her magazine, like nothing ever happened.

My eyes burned as I imagined myself snatching that magazine from her grasp and smacking her with it. I wanted more than anything to unleash all my frustrations and knock some sense into her for having the assumption that she could speak to me however she pleased.

I cleared my throat, then began as calmly as I could under the circumstances. "First of all, my name is not Joanna, you twit."

Tabitha quickly looked up at me with confusion, as if me speaking up for myself was unbelievable.

"Who do you think you're talking to?"

she fired back, standing up from the table and walking toward me.

I didn't back down. "I'm speaking to you, *Tabitha*."

I couldn't fight her. There wasn't a doubt in my mind that she'd call the police and have me locked up. That didn't mean I couldn't give her a piece of my mind.

"And another thing. I have more education than you'll ever have. You think I really want to work in this dump you call a workplace? *Do you?* No! I'd rather be somewhere using my degree."

I took two steps toward her, until we were directly face-to-face. As she stared at me, I saw something I thought I'd never see in Tabitha's eyes; fear.

I continued to speak my mind, "Don't you ever in your life speak to me like that again. *I promise you, you will regret it!*"

She took a step back, clearly knowing what was best for her. "Joanna, calm, calm down. Please."

"My name is not Joanna!" I snapped, with anger rising a couple more notches. "What am I doing here? Why am I doing this to myself? I've worked too hard in life to ever take ten steps backward and work in a place like this."

"We, we can work with you," Tabitha stammered. "We can talk this out. Just don't do something you'll regret."

I flung my hands up in frustration. "Something I'll regret? Regret? I regret ever accepting this job. I regret ever wasting my time here."

She nodded her head, then nervously looked around.

We were all alone.

No one there to witness my insanity.

I had reached my peak with that dreadful job and Tabitha's rude behavior. I was heated with no sign of calming down. Just staring at her face made me sick to my stomach. And in the heat of all that madness, I decided I couldn't do it any longer. I refused.

"I quit," I finally stated.

Tabitha blinked several times, then shook her head. If she didn't want to believe it, she'd get the picture as I walked away.

"Wait!" she called after me. "Don't go."

Tabitha rushed past me and blocked the door. She was terrified because deep down inside she knew I was a hard worker...when there actually was work to do. And worst of all, I was departing on one of the craziest days of the store's existence. They needed me.

"Tabitha, move."

"Please, Joy, you can't leave us like this."

Funny how she finally got my name right when I decided it was time to leave and never return.

"I can...and I will. Now move."

She reached out to touch my shoulder. Displeased, I gave her a look that warned her not to put her hands on me.

Quickly, she removed her hand and pleaded, "Please, don't do this to me. I'm begging you. My father will kill me when he finds out someone quit on a day like today."

I gave her the most nonchalant stare and replied, "Do I look concerned about any of that? I'm done."

I gently nudged her to the side and walked out of the break room.

As I returned to the floor and made way for the exit, I felt empowered. Fearless. Unstoppable. Like I was freaking Wonder Woman or some important female superhero.

I was on a natural high; a high I hadn't felt in quite some time. Nothing was going to bring me down at that moment. I had taken back my power and it was going to remain that way.

Being so caught up in the moment and my emotions, I wasn't looking where I was going. I bumped into someone, causing their belongings to go crashing to the floor.

"Oh, I apologize," I immediately stated, bending down to pick up the toys.

There was a laugh, followed by, "It's fine. You didn't see me. You were too busy in your thoughts, again."

I looked up to a very familiar face as he bent down to assist me. I couldn't place who he was at first, but when he smiled, I instantly remembered.

"Nick?"

He nodded, then stood, as I did as well.

"What are you doing here?"

He held up his arms, filled with merchandise. "Can't a guy shop?"

"Of course, of course. Sorry."

"Nothing to be sorry about."

I looked into his dreamy gray eyes and found myself losing track of my thoughts. Why was he so appealing that he made me jittery and awkward?

As an effort to not make things anymore uncomfortable, I said, "Well, I really must be going."

"Oh, are you off work now?"

I hesitated, "Um, kinda. Gotta go. See you around!"

I touched his arm, then began to scurry away. His scent hit my nostrils, which made me stop in my tracks.

Out of nowhere was an undeniable and lovely aroma of Christmas. I smiled, while inhaling the fresh scent of pine trees and gingerbread houses.

I closed my eyes and images of happy memories came to mind. I saw flashbacks of rare good times with my sister, decorating the Christmas tree with my mom, and sitting on my grandfather's lap as he told me Christmas stories about Santa Claus.

I opened my eyes and spun around to ask Nick what his plans were for later that evening.

But Nick was gone.

He vanished in the blink of an eye.

I couldn't place where he could've gone so suddenly, but I didn't have the time to wonder about him.

Reality had begun to sink in. I really did just quit my job. I lost my cool and allowed a bitter, cold woman to take me out of my character and lose the only form of income I had.

I walked out of that store defeated. I had no idea what to do from there.

3:04 P.M.

I drove around for hours, without a destination in mind. I didn't have gas to waste, but I also didn't want to go to my mom's and have to explain why I wasn't at work.

I couldn't handle having to face her and confess how I'd allowed my anger to get the best of me. And I was too darn prideful to return to Tabitha and ask for my job back. After how I told her off, she probably already had my photo posted on all the doors and walls, banning me from ever entering those doors.

I ended up at a park at least an hour away from town. I found a bench to sit upon and just stared off at nothing in particular. My thoughts were invading my mind too much for me to pay attention to anything else.

Thoughts of JJ and how I'd failed him wouldn't leave my mind. I was a horrible mother. Good mothers didn't just quit their jobs when they had a child to nurture and feed. Good mothers thought about every action and outcome before they did anything life changing. If I'd been a more responsible mother, none of the events that occurred that day would've been reality.

But that was my truth. I was jobless on Christmas Eve.

My heart ached and for the first time in a long time, I allowed tears to fall from my eyes, without a care in the world who saw.

7:25 P.M.

I sat outside of my parents' house for at least fifteen minutes before Mama called my cell for the fifth time within the past hour. I pondered on the idea of answering, and then decided against it. She knew I was parked outside anyway. Not a single thing went on inside or outside Barbara Carter's home without her knowledge of it.

Sucking up my pride, I got out of the car. Eying my sister's red convertible, I was aware this would be an awkward moment between us. I hadn't heard a word from her since I'd hung up on her and she hadn't heard a peep out of me either.

Mama opened the door before I could knock.

"It's about time you got out of the car." She paused, glanced me over, then asked, "What's wrong? Do you want to talk before you come inside?"

"No," I stated rather quickly. "I'm fine."

She nodded her head, but I knew she didn't believe the lies that escaped from my mouth. "Come on inside then. It's cold out here."

I entered the warm house that was filled with the aroma of baked homemade apple pies. Instantly, I thought about Nick and how just being in his presence for a few seconds, could bring out such fond childhood memories, like baking pies and sweets with Mama on Christmas Eve. As wonderful of a guy he seemed to be, there was something odd about him. I just couldn't figure it out.

"Heyyy, Daddy," I said, entering the living room and leaning over to give him a hug.

My sister sat on the other end of the couch. She glared at me, then focused on the television. That was cool with me. If she didn't want to speak, we didn't have to.

I glanced her over from head to toe and wondered if she'd gone through some hard times as well. Ebony and I looked very much alike, so alike that we were at times mistaken as twins, despite the gap in our ages. But at that time and place, we barely looked related.

I hadn't seen my sister in months, but the first thing I picked up on was her weight gain. It wasn't out of the usual for Ebony to put on a few pounds during the holidays. This time of year was extremely stressful because her daughters preferred to spend Christmas with their father and his new wife. That was perfectly understandable. But the woman sitting a few feet away from me was almost unrecognizable.

She wore blue contacts that did nothing at all to enhance her facial features. A matted black wig that was cut into what looked like a bob, covered the gorgeous red hair she hated. And if all of that wasn't enough to make her look ridiculous, she wore a fitted skirt that was not at all flattering to the fifty plus pounds she'd packed on.

Ebony needed help. But she wasn't about to get it from me.

JJ sat on the floor with his head buried into his video game. He didn't even notice I'd entered the room.

"Well, hey there," I said, getting down on the floor with him, pulling him in for a hug and a kiss.

"Hey, Mommy." He still refused to look up from his game.

"Is this the kind of warm greeting you give your mother after not seeing her all day?"

He sighed, as if being disturbed was the worst thing ever. I found it be comical.

"I love you, Mommy." He kissed my cheek and then dived right back into the game.

Whatever he was playing didn't appear to be anything I'd purchased for him. There was too much shooting and blood splattering to ever be something I'd think to put in my child's hands. And there were awful curse words I'd never expose him to. No, I surely had not made that purchase.

I picked up the case that was conveniently on the floor next to him.

"What on earth is this?" I asked, reading the case of a game entitled, "Blood Wars".

"Auntie brought it for me," he said, excitedly, looking up from the game. "And she brought me all of that, too!"

He pointed toward a big stack of presents in the corner, all different shapes and sizes. They made the tiny stack under my own tree look pitiful.

"But she told me not to open the rest until I get up tomorrow. Thank you, Aunt Ebony!"

JJ rushed over to her and gave her the warm hug he should've saved for me when I entered the room. My sister eyed me with a devilish grin, then kissed JJ's cheek.

"Anything for you, baby," she said, sweetly. "Anything at all for you."

JJ sat back down on the floor, blind to the harsh glares we were throwing back at one another. My dad, on the other hand, didn't miss a beat.

"Joy, now I think you should-"

"Don't worry, Daddy. I got this," I told him, before getting up from the floor. "Come on, Sis. Let's have a chat."

I didn't wait for her to respond. I just exited the room, hearing Daddy blurt out, "Oh gosh".

As I entered the hallway, I quickly

scanned the family photos framed on the wall. They all consisted of me, Daddy, Mama, and Ebony at happier times in our lives. That was so many years ago. I couldn't imagine things between Ebony and I ever becoming as blissful as they were in the past.

She followed me into the hallway, then with the fakest smile I've ever seen in my life, said, "What's the issue, Sis?"

What's the issue, Sis? What's the issue?

I couldn't figure out why people found it so humorous to try my patience that day. I was growing tired of it.

"You don't seem to understand my point," I began, ready to break it down as much as I had to in order to get my point across. "Say you actually had custody of your kids…"

That was hit below the belt. It cut her deep to her soul.

I resumed anyway, "And they live with you. You feed them, make sure they have everything they need. But you're personally in a financial rut and you can only afford the basic necessities."

She held up her hand and smacked her teeth. "First of all, I am not in a financial rut and I never will be. You can never compare yourself to me because although we may be related, we are not on the same level, dear heart."

I longed to smack her, pull her hair, and fight how we used to before I'd given birth to JJ.

But with my son in the other room, I fought every urge to give in to violence. Mama and Daddy would've been absolutely livid if they had to break up a fight between two grown women.

I decided to reframe from swinging and instead dig deep with the power of my words.

"I'm sorry, but if you would like to talk about levels, let's go there. Who has the college degree? Who actually works for a living instead of relying on men to pay her bills? Who actually takes care of her offspring instead of just giving up and allowing a no-good man raise them?"

She was silent. And her silence spoke volumes.

I was sure she was hot and ready to fight me. She would never throw the first punch though. No, she had to keep up her goody-two-shoes appearance for Mama and Daddy.

I didn't stop there, though. I had a few more things to get off my chest before I'd be completely satisfied.

"I get why you're so upset with me, why you've been angry for so many years. But you're grown, Ebony. You need to get over it."

"You're crazy, Joy. We are done."

She attempted to walk away, but I grabbed her arm and held on tight. She was going to listen to every word until I finished.

"You know exactly what I'm talking about. All my life you've always treated me differently. You've treated our cousins as sisters more than me."

"Joy, stop this. I don't have time for this little pity party."

My fingernails dug deeper into her arm. "No, you're going to listen. You've been angry with me for years...all because you think I had it so much easier than you growing up. All that anger because they were able to help pay for my education and not yours. All because I-"

"Joy, stop it!" she cried, with her eyes watering up.

I had not seen tears in her eyes in years. Not since our beloved grandpa passed away seven years prior.

"What's going on in here?" Mama asked, rushing into the hallway, with Daddy right behind her.

They looked at me, then to Ebony and then back to me.

"*Joyyyy*, what did you do?" Mama questioned, removing my grip on Ebony's arm.

"Why do you think I did something?"

She just gave me a glare, then passed a sympathetic look toward Ebony.

I was so over it. I was over the entire day. I needed to take my baby and go home to a place where I knew no one could bother me.

"Just don't you ever again, in your life, pull a stunt like what you did tonight. You are not JJ's mother. You've never brought him a single thing for Christmas, so why would you go all out and buy him so much now? To make me look bad, that's why. Because you know there's barely anything under our tree at home."

"Joy," Daddy said in a low tone.

Everyone now had tears in their eyes. We were a hot mess and I wasn't going to be a part of it anymore.

I rushed out of there with JJ by the hand. He cried out for his left behind presents and my parents called after me, insisting for me to stay; to work through our problems.

Our issues were too deep though. It'd take more than one night to just tap through the surface of our insanity.

9:17 P.M.

After the fourth call from Mama, I finally answered. I was relaxing in the tub, trying to soak the stress away with a third glass of champagne and bubbles filled to the rim of the tub.

"About time you finally answered," she huffed. "I been trying to call you, Joy."

"So, I noticed," I said rather harshly, with the wine really beginning to settle into my system.

She ignored my sly comment and continued on with what she had to say, "We need to discuss what happened tonight. You know your sister is sensitive. She isn't as strong as you are."

She paused to see if I had anything to add. I had no words. I'd grown tired of her and everyone saying I needed to spare Ebony's feelings because she'd been through such an ordeal. Ebony didn't care about my feelings. All of that was evident from the stunt she'd just pulled.

I swallowed the entirety of the champagne and replied, "Uh huh."

"Well, you appear to be too busy to speak

right now, so I'll let you go. We can talk about this during Christmas dinner tomorrow."

"I won't be there tomorrow, Mother. If you would like JJ there, I'll drop him off for a few hours. But do not expect me there."

"What do you mean you won't be there? It's our family tradition. Everyone will be there. All your aunts and uncles. Cousin Diane is coming down from Florida. Literally everyone is stopping by.

Ever since I could remember, the family all came together to feast in Christmas dinner at my parents' home. We had the biggest house out of all my relatives, so it only made sense to have it there. My aunts brought their signature home-made dishes, while my uncles drank beer and watched television with my father.

Those were good times. But this year would be different. I was firm in sticking with my decision. I would not be there.

"Well, everyone but me," I stated, nonchalantly.

She paused, then said, "Whatever, girl. I'll see you tomorrow."

"No, you will not, Mother."

"Joy Carter. Why are you being like this? I don't understand."

I cut her off because I didn't see the logic in pressing on with the conversation. "I gotta go, Mama. Merry Christmas."

I ended the call before she could urge me

to change my mind. She'd surely give me hell later. That was the least of my concerns. At that moment, what I really needed was another drink.

DECEMBER 25th

1:01 A.M.

When I finally did get to sleep, I was out like a light. Lately, it'd been so difficult to get a full night's rest without waking up in the middle of the night. All of that champagne really did the trick.

At least it did until a loud crash woke me up. I jolted up, scanned the dark room, and breathed a sigh of relief when I confirmed JJ was sound asleep beside me. I listened for a few seconds and only heard the beauty of pure silence.

Convinced that it was simply a bad dream and I couldn't recall or just the champagne playing tricks on me, I laid back down. I closed my eyes, ready to tackle at least a few more hours of sleep before JJ woke up.

But there was that noise again. This time it seemed louder than before and it came from downstairs.

I hopped out of bed, retrieved my bat from underneath the bed, and slowly inched toward the bedroom door. Placing an ear to the door, I listened for any footsteps or disturbances. I heard absolutely nothing.

But I definitely was not crazy.

There was something or someone in my house. And I was going to find out what was going on.

Glancing back at JJ, I was thankful he slept like a rock. I didn't need him witnessing whatever was about to go down.

This was one of the very few moments that made me wish there was a man around the house. I would've been able to hide behind my brave warrior as he stepped out into the unknown.

Snap out of it, I told myself, tiptoeing out of the bedroom and gently shutting the door behind me. There was no time for daydreaming and wishing for a man who wasn't going to show up. There were more pressing matters to attend to.

I inched down the stairs, slowly, ensuring I stepped over one of the loud, creaky steps. Silently, I swore at myself for not getting that step fixed before I lost my job. We lived in an old house that was built well before I was born. It was elegant on both the inside and out, but there was always something that needed to be fixed.

I made it down the stairs and followed the noises until I ended up standing outside of the living room.

Why me? Of all the days of the year, why

must I deal with this on Christmas?

I'd already figured out that it was a burglar breaking in to steal the already small amount of presents underneath the Christmas tree. I lived in a superb neighborhood. Why were there people breaking into homes when we all lived established lives? No one was stealing anything from my home though. Not without a fight.

With the bat resting on my shoulder, I took a deep sigh, then spun around the corner with a vengeance.

I almost dropped the bat from the shock of what I saw.

Right in front of my Christmas tree was a tall figure dressed in a quite interesting Santa suit. Like any Santa get up, it was red, but I'd never seen any as unique.

The two-piece suit fit him snug like a glove, not at all like those big and bulky Santa suits you see guys sport in the mall. There was a hood attached to the top, disguising the back of his head. The signature black boots and a black belt wrapped around his waist completed the look.

He was most definitely stylish. I wasn't sure why though. It didn't take all of that to rob a house.

I continued observing the crooked Santa and noticed he appeared to be well-built, even from behind. This made me assume he'd broken out of jail or something, and my home had been one of the first on his hit list. It was surely going to be a difficult fight trying to take down his beefy stature.

He began to hum some unrecognizable jingle as he bent over to dig into a huge velvety bag placed on the floor.

This was my chance to go for it, so I slowly crept up behind him until I was hovering over him. If I aimed directly for his head with enough force, I'd be able to knock him out long enough to tie him up until the police arrived.

Just as I was about to swing, he spoke up and said, "I wouldn't do that if I were you."

It took a second to mentally process what he'd said. How dare he break into my home, steal gifts from under my tree and still have the nerve to tell me not to knock him out. Was he warning me because he was packing some type of loaded weapon in that huge bag of his?

He could try all he wanted. I was determined to strike first. I had a kid upstairs that needed me.

I shut my eyes and swung with all my might.

But something prevented me from making contact with his head. I opened my eyes and gasped when I realized my body was stuck frozen. I couldn't move a muscle!

Panic took over as I began to wonder what was going on. I had to be dreaming. I had to be.

"Wake up, Joy! Wake up!" I began to shriek.

He replied to my outbursts in a calm tone, "This isn't a dream, so you won't be waking up."

"Who are you? What's going on? I'm calling the police, you idiot!"

He sighed, "I've had enough. I think you need a timeout."

"A timeout? No, you need to get out of my house."

"I'm not leaving until I know you don't need me anymore."

This man is crazy, I told myself. And it clearly was all a dream because I still couldn't move. Magical incidents only occurred in dreams and movies. And as far as I knew, I wasn't in a movie either.

"You've clearly lost your mind," I told him. "I need you to leave *now*! I don't need you here and I don't even know you."

He chuckled, "Is that so, Joy?"

I instantly began to lose my mind. This episode of the Twilight Zone needed to come to an end immediately!

"How do you know my name?"

He didn't respond. He simply began to pull wrapped presents from his bag and placed them under the tree. The gifts I'd purchased were still there as well.

It made zero sense. So, his plan wasn't to steal anything? He was actually adding more presents to the tree?

I looked around for a hidden camera to see if this had all been some kind of prank. There were no cameras in sight.

"What's going on here?" I demanded. "Who are you? What kind of The Grinch mess is going on here?"

He began to hum that irritating tune again, ignoring me.

"Answer me!" I yelled, now at an ultimate panic.

"Enough!" he stated, flicking his hand out and sending my body across the room to the couch.

My eyes began to become heavy. But I was able to watch him for a few seconds as he continued to pull items for his bag.

The final words I heard him utter were, "I'm only trying to help you, Joy."

And then my eyes shut completely.

1:17 A.M.

I awoke, feeling refreshed and like I'd slept for a full eight hours. My eyes made contact with my wristwatch, which dismissed that notion. I'd barely been asleep at all.

"Mmm, pretty darn good."

I looked and frowned as the tall wanna-be Santa gobbled up the freshly baked cookies I'd made with JJ before bed.

"Those cookies are not for you," I stated, now annoyed more than anything. Was he going to go dig through my refrigerator next?

"Well, the note said they were for Santa, so…"

I rolled my eyes, then attempted to get up. My body was still unresponsive.

"You know, you're a pretty good cook, by the way. I mean, considering how you took these out the freezer and baked them."

He laughed, but in my opinion there was nothing funny.

I squinted to try and see his face, but the hood on his head darkened his entire face with a shadow. It was almost like a magical hood. I did not believe in magic and fairytales though, so I continued to convince myself I was stuck in one long, annoying dream.

I found myself continuing to tell myself that when I noticed the Christmas tree. The tree I was staring at was in no way, shape or form, the one I'd put up for display. My Christmas tree was green with multicolored lights wrapped around it to the top. This new tree was simply beyond words the most stunning tree I'd seen inside of a house.

It was completely white with red ornaments that varied from snowmen to snowflakes and porcelain balls. At the very top was a star that appeared to made out of shiny and bright diamonds. I assured myself that couldn't be what I actually saw.

None of it could be reality.

"Joy, you need to wake up, girl. Wake up!"

He laughed, "I already told you. There's no waking up. This is reality."

I went ahead and entertained his idea. I figured I might as well, since I was stuck on the couch with no way out. Maybe if I played along, he'd set me free. Then I could somehow knock him out with my bat.

My eyes scanned around the room. No bat in sight.

However, I did notice my cell phone on the table in front of me. Good thing I'd drunkenly left it downstairs. I just needed him to free me and then dial 911.

"Oh, looking for this?" he asked, as the bat appeared out of thin air in his hand.

"What the-" was all I could say as I watched the bat disappear just as quickly as it appeared.

"You won't be needing that, I promise you. It isn't right to harm someone who's only trying to help, right?"

There he went again using that word "help". How was he helping me? By breaking in, eating my cookies, and holding me hostage in my very own living room?

I faked a laugh. "And how are you helping me?"

He simply gestured toward the bottom of the Christmas tree. "I've been busy while you were napping."

I closed my eyes, then opened them again to ensure my eyes were not deceiving me. Under the tree were a plethora of gifts, all wrapped in matching white wrapping paper with a red ribbon wrapped around them. There had to be at least thirty or so presents there.

"And I placed the very best...the ones from the heart...on top," he stated, referring to my small stack of presents, placed on top of his.

Stunned and amazed by the beautiful sight, I said, "You, you did all of this?"

He nodded.

"But why?"

I told you. I'm here to help," he replied, as

he grabbed the glass of milk and brought it to his head.

I watched in fascination as the contents of the glass disappeared into the darkened opening of the hood.

"Help, huh? Help me understand why you'd feel the need to help me? I don't need it."

"Is that so?"

"Yes, I know me better than anyone else does. And I know that I do not need help from you."

"So, you'd prefer I take away all these gifts...and toys for JJ?"

How does he know my son's name?
Why does he have toys for him?
Who the heck is this strange man?

"Who are you? And don't you dare say Santa Claus. I've never heard of any Santa too afraid to show his face."

"I don't know if you can handle all of that, Joy."

I rolled my eyes. "You're trespassing in my home. I think I do deserve to know who you are. That's the least you can do."

He hesitated for a moment, then said, "Okay, I can reveal myself to you. But only if you *promise* not to freak out."

"Okay, I can promise that."

"I'm serious. If you freak out and threaten to call the police or scream, I'm putting you back to sleep until I leave."

Now I found myself even more intrigued. He figured I would lose my cool after just one glance, so it made me wonder if I actually did know him. But I also didn't know anyone who could break into a home without breaking any windows or anyone who used spells, magic, or whatever it was he used, to put people to sleep.

Or did I?

"I promise," I finally stated. "I'll remain calm."

He became silent, slowly bringing his hands to the top of his head. He seemed to be moving in super slow motion, and it only made my anticipation rise.

"Take it off, please."

And off went his hood.

We stared at each other. He gave me a blank expression, while I studied his face.

Dreamy gray eyes.

Full lips.

Freshly cut hair with a full beard that connected his jawline and cheeks.

He smirked, and then I realized exactly who he was. But it made no sense. How?

"What...how are you? What?"

I shook my head, unable to believe it. I closed my eyes, then opened them to realize nothing at all had changed. It was still the exact same man staring back at me.

Tall, dark, handsome, built, and more charming than ever in that Santa suit.

"Nick?"

He nodded, then slowly walked toward me, as though he were cautious I'd overreact.

"It's me," he stated, joining me on the couch.

"How are you here? How did you get in? Why are you here?"

"I already told you why I'm here, Joy. I've been watching you for some time now."

"Obviously, you have," I snapped, not giving a care in the world about the promise I'd made a few moments before. "You're obviously crazy as well. Nick, I need for you to get out of my house…immediately."

He shook his head. "Not going anywhere."

"I'm sorry. Are you having trouble comprehending? You need to leave! You are not welcome here. You have five seconds to get out or I'm calling the police."

He stared at me, then said, "And how are you planning to do that? You can't move."

"I'll scream for JJ."

He smirked. "Good luck. You know he won't hear you. That boy sleeps too hard. Always have."

Now this was becoming freakier by the minute. He knew things there was no way he could've known. I'd never brought up my son in our previous conversations. And I didn't recall ever mentioning JJ's sleeping habits to anyone, so he literally had to have been watching us both.

"I know you must have so many questions for me, don't you?"

"You're darn right, I do! This makes absolutely not one lick of sense."

"I'll explain everything to you."

"Okay…get to it then."

He held out his hand and a folded piece of paper appeared. I watched as he unfolded it, curious to see what it might say.

"Does this look familiar?" he asked, placing it upon my lap.

I immediately knew from the messy handwriting that it was JJ's Christmas list.

"How did you get this? Explain."

Out of thin air, he retrieved an envelope that had one word written on it; Santa.

"Does all this magic not turn on any lightbulbs in your head, Joy? I just magically gave you your son's Christmas list, which you didn't even bother to read. You just took it from him and promised to give it to Santa."

I lowered my head. Work and stress had been my excuse for not opening that envelope after JJ gave it to me. I wasn't even sure how Nick managed to get it, since the last place I left it was in my nightstand drawer.

"Go ahead and read that list to me, Joy."

For the first time, I closely examined the list.

"Okay…number one, the Amega X." I looked up from the letter and said, "No surprise there. I think everyone knows how much he wants it."

"Go on, continue." He propped his feet up on the table and folded his arms above his head.

He was making himself a bit too comfortable for my liking, but I continued, "Number two…I want to meet my daddy."

Instantly, I could feel my eyes become watery. I was beginning to wish I hadn't started reading the letter.

"Number three…I want my mommy to be happy again. She's always so sad."

I closed my eyes, as a single tear rolled down my cheek.

"It's okay. You needed to read this," Nick replied, touching my hand.

Although I was still unable to move, his touch did bring a sense of comfort to me.

Looking back down at the letter, I noticed there were only three things on JJ's list. All he wanted was for me to get that darn console and I failed him. There was no way possible for me to get his father to do the right thing either.

"I'm the worst mother ever," I cried, breaking down into tears.

"No, no, no," Nick spoke gently, pulling my body toward him for an embrace. I could feel whatever force he placed on me vanish as I became able to move my limbs.

"This year is absolutely the worst!"

"It's been hard, I know. You've still managed to keep food on your table...a home for your son. That's enough right there to be proud of, Joy."

"But it isn't enough," I whined, as the tears continued to fall.

That didn't stop him from comforting me. "But it is enough. And that's why I'm here...to help make this Christmas more manageable for you."

With a touch of his finger to my cheeks, my tears instantly dried. He continued to hold me until I was able to calm down and return to my senses, which did not take long.

"Oh, I'm so sorry," I stated, moving further away from him on the couch. "I don't know what came over me."

"It's that pride of yours, again," he said, through a smirk. "Don't let a soul see you cry and it still kills you to show a single sign of weakness."

He knew me. Apparently, he knew everything there was to know about both me and my son.

As I steadily looked into his eyes, I began to feel that Christmassy-happy feeling all over again. Maybe that explained why I felt those feel-good emotions around him. Maybe he actually was...Santa?

I screamed and fell onto the floor when I heard something thump on the ceiling. "What is that? Another Santa?"

Nick laughed, then stood and grabbed my hand. As he pulled me up to my feet, he said, "Haven't you ever heard of reindeer?"

I shook my head. "No way!"

"If you don't believe all this by now, then I'm afraid you never will. Come with me."

1:30 A.M.

Nick grabbed ahold of my other hand and in a matter of seconds we zapped from my living room and onto the roof.

"Oh my!" I exclaimed, attempting to catch my breath.

It felt like my body had just gone through several hurdles. With hazy vision and lightheadedness, I leaned up against the chimney for support.

"Are you okay? Sorry, I should've warned you. Transporting by magic can be a bit overwhelming, at first."

"I'll be fine. Let's just not do that again," I stated, stepping forward to test my balance. The side effects were quickly wearing off. "How did you do that anyway?"

He gave me a look that explained how exhausted he'd become of me asking so many questions.

Instead of replying to my question, he used his hand to gesture to our right, "And here you have it. Reindeer in the flesh."

My attention spanned from Nick to the reindeer.

It was one thing to read about reindeer in books and see them in Christmas movies. But being able to see they actually did exist and were right in front of me was absolutely magnificent.

They were giant; much bigger than I ever would've imagined, and as black as coal. It might sound like an exaggeration, but they at least had to be eight or nine feet tall. Reindeer that tall could crush a tiny thing like me in a matter of seconds.

Afraid to make any sudden movements toward them, I just observed from a distance. Right before my very own eyes were eight reindeer, lined up by twos, and connected to a giant red sleigh.

That sleigh was something else. Enormous, just like the reindeer. Tiny diamonds outlined the corners of it and from where I was standing, it appeared to have a green interior. Talk about fancy!

"Why are your reindeer so…huge?"

"Why not? You see how big that sleigh is, and you saw my huge bag of goodies inside. Those puny reindeer you see in movies wouldn't stand a chance carrying so much weight."

I agreed with his logic. It was all still mighty insane and ludicrous, but I still planned to go along with it.

"Um, speaking of that sleigh and it being heavy," I stated nervously. "It won't-"

"No," he replied, shaking his head. "You

have my word that your roof will be fine."

Relieved, I asked, "So, which one is Rudolph? I don't see his red nose anywhere."

"Rudolph?" he asked, in a way that seemed surprised I even asked.

"Yeah, you can't have reindeer without Rudolph, right?"

Shaking his head, he looked at me in disbelief, then walked over to one of the reindeer in the front. "Can you believe she's looking for Rudolph, Hero?"

The reindeer looked at me and I know this sounds crazy, but I could've sworn it laughed at me.

"Hero? What kind of name is that for a reindeer?"

Hero huffed and then began to stomp his legs so hard, I feared he'd step through the roof.

"Hey, watch it," Nick warned, placing both hands on the reindeer's face, in an effort to relax him. "I told you about your temper. Can't take you anywhere without you losing control, can I?"

I observed his interaction with Hero. It was mesmerizing how he could tame him, especially with Hero being so much taller and outweighing him.

"Sorry about that," he apologized, when he returned to me. "He's a little sensitive sometimes...especially when people pick on his name. I gave it to him, years ago when I was about four years old."

"You did what?"

The more information Nick dished out about the fantasy world we were in, the more confused I became. First off, Santa had no reindeer by the name of Hero. And secondly, how old was Nick to begin with?

"This could take all night," he sighed, with a laugh.

"Just give me the SparkNotes version then."

"The what?"

I suddenly realized he for sure wasn't accustomed to sites like SparkNotes or anything an average person would be aware of, for that matter. He was...unlike anyone I'd ever met before.

"SparkNotes. It's like a...oh, never mind. Just tell me the short version."

"Oh, okay. I see. Well, just forget everything you think you know about Santa and reindeer. All that's fiction. Yes, there's the sleigh, the reindeer, the presents, but that's just the surface of it all. I won't dig into all of that because then you'll really think I'm crazy."

"Crazier than what I already think you are?" I joked. "That's not at all possible."

He laughed at my humor, then continued. "There's no Rudolph. Well, there was at some point. But that was many, many years ago. He's long been dead."

Hearing that was more than enough to make any child burst into tears. The words death and reindeer just did not belong in the same sentence.

"So, Rudolph is dead?" I questioned, unable to grasp the concept of what he was saying.

"Yes, gone. Dead. No longer living."

"And what about Cupid, Blitzen, Dasher, Dancer, and all the others? Are they all gone too?"

There was that reindeer laughter again, and this time it was from all of them.

"I think they like you. They never laugh at anyone really, but me."

"I'm flattered," I said, unsure if I really was or not. I didn't enjoy the thought of being laughed at, even if it were by reindeer.

"And yes, what you're looking at now are all of their descendants."

"You mean to tell me they had babies and this is them?"

"Yep," he replied, with a nod. "But more like their great, great, great, great, great children. And the same goes for Santa Claus."

"You mean to tell me you aren't the original Santa?"

Nick and the reindeer found humor in that question as well. I was becoming prepared to stop asking questions all together.

"No, I'm not the original Santa. And I

prefer you call me Nick. Santa is so…old, outdated, and not at all how I'd describe myself. I have style. Every Santa before me didn't."

I looked him up and down and agreed with that statement. He was too hot for me to ever place him in a category with an old guy who sported a white beard and huge belly.

"Where did that costume come from, anyway? You create it with…magic?"

"Nope. My elves designed and made it for me. It's hand stitched."

He twirled around for me, flexing his chiseled arms, pulling up his shirt to show his flat abs that were accompanied with a V-cut on each side.

"Okay, okay," I said, through laughter. "I get it. You're a hot Santa."

I tried to pretend his little show didn't impress me. But my laughter and I'm sure my super red cheeks, must've given him a hint I was amused and enjoyed the display.

"Okay, let's go. We can talk on the ride."

His body began to float up into the air. I stood there confused, until I began to float as well.

"Wait, what are you doing? We're taking a ride on that thing?"

"We sure are!" he stated, with much enthusiasm as we were seated into the sleigh. "Unless you're too afraid. And if you are, I totally understand."

"As if!" I exclaimed. "Let's do this!"

1:37 A.M.

Not even ten seconds off the ground and I already felt sick to my stomach. I was determined to hold it all together though. Throwing up was not an option.

"Are you okay? Do you need to go lie down?" he asked, touching my arm, oh so gently.

I shook my head. "No, I'm fine. Let's go."

He studied my face, ensured that I meant what I said, and then tugged onto the diamond-encrusted black reins. I fell all the way back into the seat and against Nick's arm as the sleigh took off with speed. Too much speed, if you ask me.

"Ever heard of going slow?" I asked, closing my eyes with fear of losing a contact lens from an eye.

"Nope. I only know fast and faster," he laughed.

We soared on up and reached the clouds in a mere few seconds. Truthfully, it felt like an awful rollercoaster ride.

My discomfort became transparent to Nick, as he slowed the reindeer down to a steady pace.

"You can open your eyes now."

I opened them, realized how tight I was holding onto Nick's arm, and then quickly slid over to the other side of the sleigh.

A chill came over me, causing me to shiver. I hated the cold enough already. The gush of wind, along with the thin fabric of my pajamas and t-shirt, did nothing to help the situation.

Nick was right on it before I could complain about the cold night air.

I looked down and found myself astonished by the blanket that magically appeared, covering me from my neck to feet. It was warm and cozy, replacing every goose bump and chill.

"Thank you," I said, with a tiny smile.

"Of course. You seemed…a little uncomfortable. And that's not what this should be at all. It should be fun. You need some of that in your life, you know."

I quickly defended myself. "I'll have you know that I have plenty of fun."

"Oh…not from what I've seen."

"And how exactly do you see what I'm doing? Do you have cameras at the North Pole or something?"

We shared a laugh, then he stated, "That's top-secret information. I'd get in big trouble if I told you any of that."

"You? In trouble? But you're jolly ole' Saint Nick. I would like to think you run all the rules down at the North Pole. Well, you or Mrs. Claus."

"There definitely is no Mrs. Claus," he laughed.

"No?"

"No, but I am keeping my eyes *wide open* to find her."

He gazed at me with a sly grin that made me blush and look away into the darkened sky. I could tell Nick had no problem using his charm to make women smile. If he wasn't who he was, with the giant reindeer and magical powers, I probably would've entertained the thought of dating him.

"I'm sure you'll run into her eventually."

"Bet. That is if I haven't already."

There he was again bringing a smile to my lips. I wasn't falling for it. I kept the conversation moving. "So, what else could you get in trouble for back at the North Pole?"

I looked over at him to see him deep in thought. There was nothing he could possibly do to make himself appear unattractive. He glowed with charisma and charm.

"Well, I know I shouldn't have you on this sleigh. This is a precious family heirloom, so no one but Santa, and occasionally a few elves, can be on here...unless it's an emergency. It's actually one of the most important rules."

Daryl-Jarod

"Oh, and who would you get in trouble with?"

"My dad for one...the council. Enough about that. We'll only be up here for a few moments. And I consider this to be an emergency, anyway. I'm sure they'd see things my way."

"Woah, is my life that messed up?"

"That's not at all what I meant. I just knew you needed help this year. I could sense your pain, all your frustration, the pride. If you kept going the way you were, you were going to harm yourself."

I agreed, "You're right. This year, it just seemed to be one thing after another. I didn't know how to handle it all."

"And that's why I'm here."

"To help," we said together in laugher.

"So, let me get this straight," I said, changing the subject, so I'd avoid reminiscing over the crazy year I had. "You've never taken anyone on a sleigh ride before?"

He shook his head.

"I think I feel flattered."

"I think you should be," he replied, with a wink.

"And you mentioned your dad. I know this may come off a little rude, but I never imagined Santa to have a father."

"Remember I told you to forget everything you *think* you know. Don't we all have fathers, whether we know them or not?"

I thought about JJ and how he had no idea what his dad looked like. I nodded in agreement, silently urging him to continue.

"This is how it works. When a Santa becomes too old and tired to work, he retires and lets his first-born son take over. And it goes on and on and on. No one lives forever, no matter how much magic we may have."

"Interesting, very interesting. And how many siblings do you have?"

"There are twenty of us."

"Twenty?"

"Yes!" he laughed. "Dad wasn't a big believer in having only one Mrs. Claus."

"Oh, gracious."

"And you? You have only one sister, right? Ebony?"

It felt a tad bit awkward answering any questions about myself. He seemed to already know everything there was to know. It only appeared to be a waste of breath to entertain his questions.

"Yes, but you already know this, Nick."

"I did. But I wanted to hear it from you. I do know a lot about you, but I'm unable to hear your thoughts or feel your emotions. Those are private and belong to only you."

"Hmm…" I said, now relieved Mr.-know-it-all didn't know every single detail.

"Tell me about your sister."

I rolled my eyes. "There isn't much to tell. She's my sister and we don't get along."

"And why is that?"

"Did we come up here for a therapy session? I honestly prefer we not talk about her."

"That's fair. Just know that things are changing for the better in your life. You could wake up with everything turned around. You just have to let go first."

"What are you talking about? Let go of what?"

He looked at me, then gave up on the conversation. I was being difficult again, pretending to not know what he meant.

He wanted me to let go. Let go of the anger I knew was bottled up deep down inside for my sister? Not likely. The wounds were too deep and I couldn't forget and forgive overnight.

For the first time since we'd been up in the air, I noticed how beautiful the sky was. We'd both been so distracted by our pleasant conversation, but now that there was a moment of silence I could thoroughly enjoy the view.

The stars and the moon shined bright that night; far more beautiful up close and personal. There was a tiny bit of fog in the night air. However, it didn't take away from the magnificent view. It was spectacular!

And although I didn't want to admit it, it was romantic as well. I allowed myself to enjoy the moment, for no one would ever be able to top the experience Nick provided.

Finally, I looked to him and asked, "Why aren't there more men like you these days? I mean, I know this sleigh ride is a once-in-a-lifetime opportunity, but men who actually care do not exist anymore. They don't care about a romantic evening, while getting to know you."

"And how do you know this?"

"I am a woman, aren't I? And let's just say I haven't had very much luck in the dating department."

"I'll be brutally honest with you," he began. "You can't say all of this if you haven't been trying. You turn down men left and right…good men. But you'd never know because you don't give them a chance. All that hurt and disappointment from the past won't let you move on and be happy."

Yikes! He had me there. And worst of all, I began to think about all the men who'd tried to take me out. I told myself they were all rude, but not *all* of them were.

Either they were too short, too tall, too skinny, not successful enough, or I just didn't like how they groomed their facial hair. I had an excuse for each and every one of them. And all because I was afraid that what happened with Jeffrey would happen with everyone else.

"Would you like to help me?" Nick asked, referring to the big bag of presents that appeared in the back of the sleigh.

"You mean, I can help you?"

"Of course. I'd love your help."

The reindeer stopped directly above the chimney of a nearby house. Nick then handed me a present, wrapped exactly like the ones he placed under my tree, with white wrapping paper and a red ribbon.

"We can do one house and then I'll take you home."

I agreed, but couldn't deny the feeling of disappointment. Strange how I was determined to whack that man in the head an hour ago and now I was eager to spend the entire night with him, if I could. I would travel with him to each and every house around the globe, just to hear more of his stories and history. But as I learned very early in life, all good things must come to an end.

"You don't expect me to go down a chimney, do you?" I asked, referring to how his reindeer stopped above the chimney.

"No, silly. I'm too fly for chimneys. Let's go."

2:05 A.M

We transported from the sleigh and into the living room of the small home.

There on the couch was a little girl, no older than JJ. She was sound asleep.

Nick placed a finger to his lips, signaling for me to be quiet. He then began to place a few presents underneath the tree. I silently observed him. He seemed very content, happy, and dedicated with what he was doing. I hoped to someday have a job I was content with as well.

He finished filling up the tree, then looked at me and down to the present in my hand. I bent down to place it under the tree, but Nick stopped me by pointing toward the sleeping child.

I shook my head out of fear I'd wake her.

"It's okay," he whispered.

I slowly approached her and gently placed it by her hand. She didn't stir a bit, which further proved Nick really knew these kids.

Nick smiled my way, then grabbed the two cookies from the table, handing me one of them. I attempted to decline, but he insisted with his eyes that I indulge.

I bit into the cookie and immediately grabbed a napkin from the table to spit it out. Nick did the same.

I stared at the little girl and shook my head. Poor baby must've baked the cookies without much supervision. At least, I hoped that was the case. Any adult who baked that horribly did not deserve to be in the kitchen.

2:09 A.M.

In the blink of an eye, we were back inside of the sleigh, finally able to laugh out loud.

"I am so sorry. The cookies are normally pretty good."

"No worries. At least she'll think Santa ate the cookies."

"Indeed, she will. That gift you placed next to her is going to make her day tomorrow."

"Oh? And what was it?"

"It's a camera. Her very first camera. Little Miranda dreams of one day becoming a photographer, but her mom was unable to buy her a camera. You just helped make that dream come true."

"That's kinda cool."

"Yeah, I guess it is. Like you."

We were back in the air in no time. As we flew by house after house at a comfortable speed, I thought back to the gift I wanted most of all as a child. It was the African American edition of the 1991 holiday Barbie. I wanted that doll just as much as JJ wanted the Amega X, if not more.

I wondered why Santa never brought me

that gift. And then I quickly recalled how naughty I'd been that year by cutting off my sister's hair as she slept.

2:22 A.M.

I'll take you inside," Nick told me, once the sleigh landed on the roof.

Silently, I was protesting we stay outside a tad bit longer, talk and get lost in conversation. But he had things to do. Who knew how many more houses he had to stop by before everyone awoke.

"Okay, sounds good."

I placed my hand in his and prepared myself for a final transport. I wasn't fearful this time. The more my body endured it, the more adjusted I became. I just did not enjoy the thought of saying goodbye.

Hero began to stomp his feet, causing a thunderous ruckus. Startled, I squeezed Nick's hand tighter and hid behind him.

"Hero," Nick warned, in a forceful, yet still calm tone. "You need to cool it."

Hero huffed and stomped a final time before falling silent.

"He doesn't want you to go," Nick laughed. "That's very interesting."

"Oh? And why is that?" I inquired, stepping out from behind him.

"Hero is my most difficult reindeer. He

doesn't like people. So, it's interesting to see he's taken a liking to you...even after you teased his name."

"Well, I like you too, Hero," I said directly to him. I then turned back to Nick and asked, "Do you mind if I...say goodbye?"

"Not at all. Be my guest."

I steadily approached Hero and stopped when I stood directly in front of him. He looked down at me and I didn't feel any of the panic or fear I'd felt during our initial meeting.

He was a black majestic beauty. All the reindeer were.

"Guys, don't look so sad," Nick teased. "If you both promise to be on your best behavior, maybe you'll see each other next Christmas."

I smiled, then wrapped my arms around Hero. He lowered his head until it rested gently on my shoulder.

He was a sweetheart. Massive and mighty, with a heart of gold.

After a few moments, I parted from our sentimental farewell and gave Nick permission to take me inside. In a flash, we were back inside the comfort of my living room.

We met in that living room, and we'd part ways in it as well.

"Don't look so sad," he told me, pulling me in for a hug.

I didn't fight it. There was no use. I would

never see him again. I might as well have allowed him to see some emotion from me.

"Do I really look sad though?" I asked, wrapping my arms around him.

"Like a kid who lost his puppy."

"Wow. That is pretty darn sad."

"What would make you happy right now, at this very moment?"

I loosened the hug and made eye contact with those dreamy eyes. What would've made me happy would be Nick staying with me. I'd never felt so comfortable with a man in all my life. No one was perfect, but he surely was one in a million.

I knew there was no way I'd get my wish, so I went for the next best thing. I pulled him toward me by his shirt and pressed my lips against his.

Not once did he tense up or push me away. Nick wanted the kiss just as much as I did. It was so hot it could warm me up on the coldest of all the winter days. It was life changing and would be historically the best kiss I'd had the pleasure of experiencing.

The kiss ended and was followed by that unstoppable eye contact. Our eyes told the story of two souls connected. Two souls that had no choice but to part.

"I'm not good with goodbyes," I confessed.

"Close your eyes."

"Why?"

He calmly repeated himself, "Close your eyes. Trust me."

I closed my eyes, hoping he'd throw me and JJ up onto his sleigh and we could ride around for eternity.

"Think about everyone who's ever disappointed you."

I peeked one eye open, giving him a puzzled look.

"Just do it. There's a reason behind it."

Just…trust…him. Trust him.

My eyes closed and I did what he asked. I focused on the one person I was the most upset with at that moment; Ebony.

"When you think of the first person, think about the incident that really pushed you over the edge. What happened that made you wish you didn't have to deal with them any longer?"

I thought about Ebony buying JJ so many gifts when she knew I wouldn't be able to do the same. But I didn't stop there. I also thought about how upset she made me on my college graduation day when she purposely ended up in the hospital to take the shine away from me. The more it flashed through my head, the more upset I became.

"Okay, now stop. You feel all that anger and disappointment?"

"Yes,"I said through clenched fists and tears.

"Now, I need you to just forget it. Forget it all."

"But I can't. She really hurt me, Nick."

He wiped away my tears. "You can't move on until you let go, love. Don't be afraid."

His voice was calm and reassuring. It assured me I should listen and I'd be just fine in the end.

"Are you letting go?"

I breathed a deep sigh. "Yes, I'm letting go."

As those words excited my mouth, I envisioned my sister and I starting over. I could see us making amends and actually putting in effort to like each other...to love each other. I smiled at just the thought of it.

"Good, good," he said, rubbing my shoulders. "Now picture that other person you're so upset with."

Jeffrey's face appeared. I became tense all over again as my mind wandered through memories of loneliness and heartache. From him showing up at the hospital and informing me the baby was not his to just all together not taking care of a child he knew for certain was his seed.

There was no love in my heart for him. Only regret.

Regret and hatred.

"Now think of that one thing that could change the situation. What would make things right?"

I thought about how JJ begged to see his father. He wanted that more than anything. Thoughts of the two of them together and bonding, gave me a sense of peace. I realized that was the one thing I wanted most in the world as well.

Nick kissed my forehead, then softly said, "Let go, Joy. Let go of all the tears. All the pain. All the disappointment. You're about to start over. This next year will be all about new and fresh memories."

He kissed my forehead, then my lips, before continuing, "Let go, Joy. Let it all go..."

8:34 A.M.

Mommy! Mommy! Wake up! It's Christmasssss! Mommy, it's Christmas!"

JJ woke me up with his loud screaming as he jumped up and down on the bed.

"JJ, baby," I said, now fully awake as I stretched. "Stop jumping before you fall."

He immediately got off the bed and begin to jump around in place. "Let's go open presents, Mommy!"

Flashbacks began to run through my head like a freight train. Nick placing all the presents under the tree. The sleigh ride. The kiss. That amazingly beautiful kiss. Had it all only been a dream?

Yes, it had to have been. What else would explain how I ended up in my bed?

It definitely was a dream…one of the best dreams of my life.

"Mommy, Mommy! Come here!"

JJ, who was no longer standing in front of me, broke me from my daydream. I hopped out of bed and followed the sound of his voice downstairs, and into the living room.

"What is it JJ? What's wro-"

I lost my train of thought as I entered the living room and stared in amazement at the Christmas tree.

There were the presents from last night. All still there, wrapped in white and red.

I glanced at the table and almost jumped for joy when I noticed the milk and cookies were gone. It all confirmed what had happened in the wee hours of the morning was all reality.

Nick was real.

Santa was real.

And I'd gone flying in the air with him and his reindeer, for an incredible ride I'd never forget.

JJ had already begun to rip into his presents and before I knew it, he was all finished. He looked over at me with tears in his eyes.

"What's wrong, baby?" I asked, rushing over to him.

"All these toys."

"What about the toys?"

He began to cry. "What I really wanted. Santa didn't bring it. He just got me all these toys."

I scanned the floor, through all the boxes and wrapping paper. I saw a variety of toys, but the Amega X was nowhere to be found.

"It's okay, JJ," I said, rubbing his back. "You still have all these toys to play with."

"But it's not what I wanted."

He pulled away from me and went to the corner to cry.

"JJ, if you don't cut it out right now! You need to be grateful for what you do have."

Way to go Nick! Are you trying to teach him he can't get everything he wants in life? It's a bit too soon for all that!

I became irritated. Irritated that Nick gave JJ some many toys when he could've just given him the one thing he wanted.

And irritated with JJ for not being content with what he was given. As a child, I'd never been so lucky. He should've been on that floor happily playing with toys. Not in a corner crying!

The ringing of my cell phone gave my brain a break from what would surely become a headache.

I glanced at it on the table and had to think twice before answering.

"Hello," I said, with not a single ounce of enthusiasm.

"Hey, Sis. Merry Christmas."

I inhaled deeply, then exhaled.

"Merry Christmas to you as well."

"Is everything good over there? Is that JJ crying?"

I looked over at JJ who hadn't stopped crying. He was heartbroken. He just knew Santa would come through for him.

"Yes, yes. Everything is fine. What's up?"

She hesitated, then went ahead with what was on her mind. "I couldn't sleep last night. I was thinking about what I did. And I truly am sorry. Can we sit down and talk later today? I seriously want to stop all of this fighting."

I pulled the phone away from my ear to make sure the contact in my phone was indeed my sister.

"Hello? You still there?"

"Yes, you caught me by surprise, that's all," I admitted, with a hand resting on my chest. "Of course, we can talk. I'd love th-"

The aggressively ringing doorbell distracted me from finishing my statement. Whoever it was wasn't the least bit patient and continued to push it repeatedly.

"Is that Santa with my Amega X?" cried JJ, running out of the room.

"Ask who it is, JJ," I called after him.

"Sounds like a lot going on over there," Ebony laughed.

"You can say that again."

"Listen, I really am sorry, Joy."

I smiled. "You don't have to say it again. I'm sorry as well. I overreacted and I, I…I."

The unexpected visitor walked into the room with a smile upon his face.

I hadn't seen him in an extended amount of time, but I'd recognize him anywhere. Looking him over, not a thing had changed except for his bald head, which he'd probably decided to sport because of his crooked hair line.

There was nothing cheap on his body, either. He was dressed from head to toe in designer and smelled like money.

"Ebony, let me, let me call you back."

I didn't even end the call. I just allowed the phone to drop from my hand and onto the floor.

"Hello there, Joy. Merry Christmas."

"Merry Christmas? How dare you show your sorry face around here?"

I ran up to him and delivered a much-deserved slap upon his face. He must've lost all his sanity to think he could show up at my door and be invited inside after what he'd done.

"Why'd you hit my daddy?" asked JJ, with worry written all over his face.

I looked from JJ to Jeffrey and could barely handle it. They looked so much alike. There was no denying JJ was his son. And that made me revert back to the day Jeffrey informed me JJ looked nothing like him and was not his.

Yes, Jeffrey's strong genes were passed down to our son, but his attitude and behavior, on the other hand, would not. It was my ultimate mission to raise my son with enough morals to differentiate between right and wrong.

I couldn't deal anymore. Christmas Day needed to be over and done with.

"I deserved that. I know," the sorry-excuse-for-a-father said with a grief-stricken face. The nerve of him to look so hurt.

"Glad you know it. Now what are you doing here? How did you know where I live?"

"Mommy, look what Daddy brought me. He does love me," JJ happily exclaimed, pushing a huge wrapped box into the room.

"I see. I see," I stated as I eyed the box, then focused back to his father. "What are you doing here, Jeffrey?"

"I, I was, I was-"

"You were what? I need an answer, like today."

Let it go, Joy.

Let it go.

Nick's voice was speaking to me, but I ignored it.

"I been feeling really bad lately, Joy. I should've stepped up a long time ago. I know I messed up and I can't turn back time."

"You're right. You can't. JJ is now a six-year-old. He didn't even know what you looked like."

Let it go.

"How did you know where I lived?"

"Your dad told me a few years ago, before I moved the last time."

"And you just decided now is the perfect time to waltz in here? What is wrong with you?"

"I mean, I've been thinking about it for some time now, Joy."

"Daddy got it for me, Mommy! Look!

Look!"

I looked over to see JJ dancing all over the room. Right there on the living room floor was the Amega X. I'd never in my life been so thrilled to see a gift. How Jeffrey knew JJ wanted it was beyond me.

"Thank you, Daddy! Thank you!" JJ exclaimed, hugging onto Jeffrey.

"You're welcome, son," Jeffrey beamed with pride.

Son? You haven't known him for five minutes and you wanna call him son?

Let. It. Go.

As the two of them embraced, I looked away. I was so disgusted I couldn't stand to look at Jeffrey's face.

Something caught my eye. Something that hadn't been there before.

I walked over to the table and picked up a large box that had an envelope attached to it. My name was written on it in a fancy gold print.

I glanced over at JJ, who was preoccupied with Jeffrey as they unboxed the Amega X. I wondered if the gift came from JJ. At first I figured that maybe my parents gave him money to purchase it, but the printed handwriting was too neat. The box was also wrapped exactly like the presents Nick left upon the tree.

I decided to find out what exactly was in

the box before opening the envelope. I tore off the ribbon and wrapping paper, then gasped when I realized it was a Barbie.

Not just any Barbie. It was the 1991 edition I begged for as a child, but never got. Attached to the packaging was a note that read: **Because You Weren't So Naughty This Year.**

I laughed at Nick's humor, admired the doll for a moment, and then placed it down as I opened the envelope.

"Oh man! I can't wait to play this!" exclaimed Jeffrey, while gazing at the beauty of the gaming console now that it was out of its box.

I rolled my eyes at the thought that he'd probably purchased it for himself.

"I'll be right back," I told them, as I slipped out the front door, with neither one of them paying attention.

I needed peace and quiet so I could read the letter, word for word, without a single distraction. JJ would be fine for a few moments with his father. Jeffrey was a lousy dad, but not crazy enough to harm his son in any way.

I sat down on the front steps and tuned everything out but the contents of the letter.

Dearest Joy,

My time spent with you has been a night I'll never forget. I was able to be myself with you...both me and my reindeer. ☺

And it's funny because my goal was to simply help you. I wanted you to see the light and realize how quickly your life can change for the better if you were able to learn one simple lesson.

Unexpectedly in return, you showed me something as well. You showed me how truly bright your light shines, inside and out. It's so beautiful and special. I wish I could be around it every day, not just on Christmas.

Anytime you need help looking beyond what people have done to you...just close your eyes...and remember to let go and give yourself the gift of moving on.

With high hopes to see you again,
Nick.

I reread the letter a few times, becoming more ecstatic each time I read it.

"What the?" I exclaimed suddenly, while examining the white sprinkles that began to fall and melt onto the letter.

I looked up in wonder, not sure if I could believe what I saw to be reality.

It was snow. But not just any regular snowfall like previous years before. This was now hard-falling snow. If it maintained at that pace, we would surely experience a winter wonderland.

There wasn't a doubt in my mind who was responsible for it. Nick had already given me so much, with the most important being Jeffrey's willingness to try and be there for JJ. I would still be cautious at first, to see if Jeffrey was one hundred percent serious. But no matter what happened with that situation, I was forever grateful to Nick.

I placed the letter to my lips for a kiss, closed my eyes, and tilted my head up to the sky.

"Thank you, Nick. Wherever you are...thank you."

A Note from the Author

Thank you for reading Santa Baby. I hope it succeeded in entertaining you, as well as bringing you some type of cheer this holiday season.

This book was initially planned out to be an erotic tale for the holidays. That quickly changed when I sat down to write it. Before I knew it, I had a novella completed within two weeks.

What I thought would be just a short eBook for the holidays, transformed into so much more as I became more invested in the characters, Joy especially. I soon found myself striving to provide a more well-rounded and romantic offering.

Writing this book was also therapeutic. I realized that I have quite a bit in common with Joy, as some of you I'm sure, can agree. In fact, I believe she's my most relatable character to date.

Here we have a woman who's so prideful she doesn't want help from anyone, not even her own parents. She'd rather suffer and struggle than reach out for a favor.

But Joy does learn one important lesson at the book's conclusion. She learns how important and beneficial it can be to let go!

How many of us hold onto hurt and despair for years, without ever considering to look past it? I'm guilty of it. And penning this book helped me see how truly necessary it is to free our minds of all things that hold us back from living fruitful and productive lives.

Once again, thanks for your support. Stay tuned for more entertaining fiction in the near future.

With Love,
Daryl-Jarod